DOES WHAT'S Right!

By Kelly Lynch   Illustrated by Casey Lynch

magic
wagon

visit us at www.abdopublishing.com

To my wife, affectionately —KL
For Maggie —CL

Published by Magic Wagon, a division of the ABDO Group, 8000 West 78th Street, Edina, Minnesota 55439. Copyright © 2011 by Abdo Consulting Group, Inc. International copyrights reserved in all countries. All rights reserved. No part of this book may be reproduced in any form without written permission from the publisher.

Looking Glass Library™ is a trademark and logo of Magic Wagon.

Printed in the United States of America, North Mankato, Minnesota.
092010
012011
♻ This book contains at least 10% recycled materials.

Written by Kelly Lynch
Illustrations by Casey Lynch
Edited by Stephanie Hedlund and Rochelle Baltzer
Cover and interior layout and design by Abbey Fitzgerald

Library of Congress Cataloging-in-Publication Data

Lynch, Kelly, 1976-
   Mighty Mike does what's right! / by Kelly Lynch ; illustrated by Casey Lynch.
     p. cm. -- (Mighty Mike)
   ISBN 978-1-61641-131-2
   [1. Repairing--Fiction. 2. Responsibility--Fiction. 3. Community life--Fiction.] I. Lynch, Casey, ill. II. Title. III. Title: Mighty Mike does what is right!
   PZ7.L9848Md 2011
   [E]--dc22
                                                        2010016155

Bringggg, bringggg. Mike grabbed the phone off his office wall and barked into the receiver, "This is Mighty Mike, the mightiest heavy equipment operator of them all. There's no job too big, no job too small. How can I help you?"

Mrs. Harper from Pullman Lane was on the other end of the line. Mrs. Harper explained that she had a leaky pipe that needed fixing pronto.

"Yep, I can do that. I'll be there first thing in the morning," Mike promised. He knew that with his big excavator, he'd have the job done in no time.

Bringggg, bringggg. As soon as Mike set down the phone, it rang again.

"This is Mighty Mike, the mightiest heavy equipment operator of them all. There's no job too big, no job too small. How can I help you?" Mike scribbled notes as he talked. "Yep, uh-huh, wow. Oh, that might be a problem. I'll have to get back to you."

Mike hung up the phone and smacked himself on top of the head. Mr. Stern of the National Pacific Intercontinental Galactic Pipeline Company needed Mike's excavator for a big job—starting tomorrow! But Mike had made a promise to Mrs. Harper. What should he do?

Mike slid back into his chair. There was sweat on his forehead. He laid his head on his desk. Then, he began to remember jobs he'd done with his big excavator.

He remembered the time that he'd used it to dig a humongous hole for a skyscraper's foundation. He was mighty proud every time he drove through the city and saw the tall steel building.

He remembered building a huge wall of boulders after the big mudslide washed out the highway. Now, the people wouldn't have to worry about mud washing out the road again.

Mike thought about the time he'd built a road all the way to the top of a mountain. The road was so the phone company could install new towers.

Mike thought about all the jobs he'd done. He'd always done his best. Mike's smile turned to a frown.

He humphed and he hemmed and he hawed as he paced around his office. *What to do?* Mike wondered.

Then, Mighty Mike's frown flipped around and turned into a smile again. "I've always kept my word," he said. "I must fix Mrs. Harper's leak, even if it means I miss out on Mr. Stern's big job."

The next morning Mike was at Mrs. Harper's house bright and early.

He dug a big hole and fixed the leak.

Then, he filled the hole back in. He had everything finished just as the sun was going down.

Mrs. Harper came out with a big smile just as Mighty Mike finished. Mike could tell she was pleased with the work he'd done. She thanked him when he had loaded his big excavator on the trailer behind his dump truck.

"No problem," said Mighty Mike as he climbed into the seat of his truck. "I'm Mighty Mike, the mightiest heavy equipment operator of them all. There's no job too big, no job too small."

Mike went back to the office knowing that he had done the right thing. He had made a promise, and the trustworthy thing to do was see it through!

Glossary

excavator - a power-operated shovel.

foundation - the underlying support structure or base of a building.

heavy equipment operator - a person who drives and uses construction machinery.

humongous - extremely large.

mudslide - a moving mass of soil caused by rain or melting snow.

pronto - without delay.

skyscraper - a very tall building.

trustworthy - a person who is dependable.

What Would Mighty Mike Do?

• What does Mighty Mike do when he is asked to do two jobs?

• Why does Mighty Mike choose to do Mrs. Harper's job?

• How does Mighty Mike feel when Mrs. Harper's job is finished?